JEEP THOMPSON & THE LOST PRINCE OF VENUS

EPISODE 1: JOURNEY TO THE SECOND PLANET

WARREN BLUHM

JEEP THOMPSON & THE LOST PRINCE OF VENUS:
Episode 1: Journey to the Second Planet
© 2023 Warren Bluhm. All rights reserved
ISBN 979-8-9863331-4-4

For a digital copy of this book, visit http://eepurl.com/LxdHT

1

ONCE UPON A TIME

Once upon a time in a land not unlike our own, there lived a young woman who wanted to see the stars.

"I gotta tell you, it's pretty darn boring around here sometimes," the young woman would say, even though her best friend, Blaine, was a vampire, which would make anyone else's life interesting.

Blaine wasn't a dangerous vampire, and that is one of the ways the land where she and Blaine lived WAS unlike our own. In this civilized land, vampires could go to the grocery store and buy pasteurized blood in bottles, some of them flavored with flavors no one ever thought of until they did, some as obvious as cherry vanilla and others not as obvious.

But about the young woman being bored: It was because her mother had been an explorer, although how much of one wasn't clear until the day they found The Traveler.

"Guinevere," Mom would say, "this is a vast and wonderful place, and there's more to reality than these four walls and the sky above."

And so the young woman wanted to see beyond these four

walls and the sky above. That's where all the trouble began, although years later she would tell people it was also where her real life began.

But she would not ever tell anyone else that her name was Guinevere. The only reason Blaine knew was because he heard Mom call her that once, earning an embarrassed roll of the eyes and a glare that would have made Mom's blood curdle if it hadn't made her laugh out loud instead.

Guinevere Prudence Thompson hated her name. Hated it. Never mind that she was named after an Arthurian queen and a Beatles song.

"Call me G.P.," she insisted one day. "I don't want to be — that name — so call me G.P. instead."

"Jeep?" asked her incredulous mother that first time.

"No! G.P."

"OK, Jeep," Mom grinned.

She told her friends just to call her G.P., too, but it wasn't long until — just like Mom and the military's "general purpose (G.P.) vehicles" before her — everyone just shortened it to Jeep. And that kind of grew on her. Eventually.

By the time her mother called her Guinevere in front of Blaine, G.P. was rather fond of the name Jeep.

"Mahhmmm," she growled in a manner that would be menacing if there was anything at all in the world that could make Mom feel menaced.

"What?" she grinned. "It's your name. It's a beautiful name."

"It may have been a beautiful name in the 14th century when you were born," Jeep said. "But my friends call me Jeep, and Blaine is my friend."

Mother had a way of laughing that could disarm a stegosaurus. It was full of music and adventure and a happiness that came from living life just the way she had always dreamed. And when she laughed, even Jeep couldn't stay furious.

"I promise, Guinevere," Blaine said, as soberly as he could manage as he struggled not to smile in the face of Jeep's fury and Mom's laughter, "I will never call you by that name."

"You just did."

"I will never call you by that name again, G.P.," he said, quietly and sincerely, for Blaine was nothing if not quiet and sincere.

Blaine was tall and round — no, he wasn't overly plump, but he had an oval face that suggested roundness all over, although his softness was simply because he didn't care to tone his body into buff — let's just say he was tall with an oval face that always looked a little sleepy. It was something about his eyes: Blaine just never seemed to have his eyes completely open, and his eyebrows could speak volumes and often did.

The other thing about Blaine is that he always seemed to have a little smile, as if he knew something funny about the most serious situations. The word for his face was droll. Yes, that's it: He had a droll face. He viewed the world with a droll outlook. Blaine was unflappable. And droll.

Jeep had long, straight red hair with a face neither too narrow nor too pudgy, not the most beautiful young woman ever, but certainly very pleasant to look at.

Her eyes were a remarkable green color, green as the ocean on a clear, bright sunny day, and they were constantly in motion, darting here and there and seeing everything there was to love about wherever she was and wherever she was going. It was odd, in fact, that she felt bored, because she was the kind of person who found life interesting all the time.

And honestly, Jeep didn't worry about what she looked like. She went about life because it was fun to be alive, and she didn't trouble herself wondering whether she was pretty or pleasant to look at. And that, truth be told, is what made her pretty.

Now, Jeep Thompson lived with her mother in a house in, as I mentioned at first breath, a land not unlike our own. Mom rarely talked about Jeep's father, but when she did, it was with a sweet smile and a faraway look that seemed to be replaying fond memories.

"No, of course not," she said one day when Jeep was 17 and asked if she ever got angry that he wasn't there. "I will always love your father."

"So where is he?" Jeep insisted, because she was in a mood where it would be nice to have a dad around and she didn't seem to have one. "Is he dead?"

Mom sighed at that. "No, he's not dead," she said. "I think I would be able to feel it if he was, if you know what I mean," but of course Jeep didn't know.

"Well, then, where is he? What happened?"

"I'm not really sure where he is," Mom admitted. "Someday, when I can, I'll tell you the whole story."

"When you can? You mean when I'm old enough to understand or something?"

Mom looked in Jeep's eyes with an expression that seemed to say that she really, really wanted to tell her the whole story right then and there.

"What, did he disappear on some top-secret mission and you're not allowed to tell me? Come on, Mom."

"Yes, he disappeared," her mother said. "And it wasn't top secret, it's not that I'm not allowed to tell you. It's that it's best I not tell you until the right time."

"That's not mysterious or anything."

It was quiet for a very long time, and then Mom repeated, "Someday, Gwin, when I can, I will tell you the whole story."

"Do you promise?"

Then Mom smiled a very, very, very strange smile and said something very odd.

"Not only do I promise," Mom said, "I already have told you the whole story."

"When?! I think I would have remembered something like that."

But Mom just kept smiling that very, very, very strange smile.

"I love you, Guinevere Prudence Thompson."

"Don't call me that!" Jeep said. "I love you, too, but I don't remember you telling me about Dad."

"I know," was all Mom said. But then, a moment later, she said something that was even odder.

"I want you to know," Mom said carefully, "that it'll be OK. You will go through so much, but you'll be OK — and I'm so sorry for what you have to do."

"What do I have to do?"

"It's a long story, and I can't tell you now, but I have already told you what you need to know as you go along."

"That doesn't make any sense at all!" Jeep said.

"Not today it doesn't," Mom agreed. "You got angry — you got very angry at first when I told you — furious, actually — but when you hear what it is, at least you'll understand."

"I don't remember any of this."

"Of course you don't, because I haven't told you yet."

"Um, going in circles a little much, Mom?"

A big, sad smile now. "You'll figure it out, I promise, and then you'll save the worlds. I'm so proud of you."

It appeared at the time, however, that Jeep would have to figure it out for herself, because shortly after her 18th birthday, her mother died.

2

MOM HAS A SECRET

Jeep never got used to the hospital bed in the living room, against the wall where the Christmas tree stood every December. Mom, who always had been full of life and energy, had aged daily, it sometimes seemed, until now she looked like a shriveled little imitation of herself lying there, hooked up to monitors with an I.V. inserted in the back of her hand to keep her hydrated or something.

The visiting nurse finished taking Mom's vital statistics, double-checked the intravenous drip, and smiled blankly at Jeep.

"Sorry to interrupt," the nurse said, a hand brushing back Mom's hair. "I'll be in the kitchen for a while before I have to go, so holler if you need me."

"Thank you," Mom said, and after the nurse was out of earshot, added to Jeep, "She's one of the good ones. I wish they were all like her."

"She does seem nice," Jeep said, although she couldn't really tell the difference between this nurse and any of the others who came to the house twice a day to monitor her mother's deterioration.

She managed to laugh at one of Jeep's lame jokes and then something dark seemed to pass over her eyes.

"Honey," Mom said, "you need to know something, something important."

"OK ..."

"Out in the garage, under the tarp —"

Jeep relaxed a little. "Yeah, Mom, what IS that thing? Some old classic car from the '70s or something?"

The woman lying in the bed widened her eyes and then laughed softly.

"You little snit," she said. "When did you look under the tarp?"

Jeep shrugged. "I don't know, it was a really long time ago. They made cars a lot bigger when you were a kid."

"Yes, they did, but it's not a classic car from the'70s. You're close, though," and Mom coughed from laughing. "The design is based on a 1965 Buick Riviera — the designer had an impish streak — but it's more than a car. Much, much more than that."

"Huh."

"We called it The Traveler," Mom said in a half-whisper. "It's how I traveled between worlds over the years."

OK. This was something new. Jeep knew Mom was involved in some sort of scientific research she wasn't allowed to talk about, and now she was talking about it. And she traveled — wait, what?

"Between worlds? Like you went to Mars?"

"And Venus, and —"

"Oh my gosh, Mom! This is ridiculous!"

"And by ridiculous you mean —"

"Awesome! You went to Venus and Mars and what was it like? Howcome you're not like famous? Why doesn't everybody know? Why is your spaceship sitting under a tarp in the garage?!"

"It wasn't as —"

"Oh, Mom," Jeep said, her eyes suddenly wet, "Why didn't you ever take me with? We could have had so much fun together."

"I know," she said, patting her daughter's hand. "But you have to be very careful. I was waiting for the right time; I guess I thought we had plenty of time."

"That's OK," Jeep said, although of course it wasn't OK. To walk with her Mom on Venus — or Mars — it would have been incredibly special.

"Like I said, you have to be very careful calibrating your settings," Mom said. "We lost your father that way."

"What? My dad went with you, too?"

"No, he went out in the first Traveler, and we lost him because we —"

"Wait. You and Dad worked together on this? You have to tell me everything!"

"Yes, I think it's time. Slow down and I'll tell you," Mom said. "What I was trying to say is you have to be careful with your calibrations when you decide where you're going — and when you're going. That's what got you in trouble."

"What does that mean? What did I do?" Jeep said. "I never did more than look at it, I swear."

"Oh, I know. It's nothing that you did, it's what you're going to do."

"No, you said that's what 'got' me in trouble, like I already did something."

Mom smiled. "Right. It's my past, your future. Oh, Gwin, I'm so proud of you."

This was now not only confusing but embarrassing. "So I'm going to get in trouble, but you're proud of me for doing it?"

"Oh, the places you'll go —"

"OK, cut it out, Dr. Suess," Jeep said, which made Mom laugh, which was good news and bad news because she hadn't laughed much lately but she started coughing and it took a minute before she could speak again.

"Oh, dear," Mom said, her eyes suddenly filling with tears.

"There's so much I want to tell you, but you have to find out for yourself. You have to go through so much, and I can't help you any more than I already have. I wish there was another way to do this, but the worlds depend on you discovering it all in the order you discovered it. Oh, my little Guinevere, a mother only wants to protect her little girl, and I can't protect you from what's going to happen. I wish I could tell you, I wish with all my heart, but I can't, I just can't."

And now Jeep's mother was sobbing.

"OK, Mom, here we go again, this is not making sense at all, and you're really starting to scare me," Jeep said, not scared for herself as much as scared that her mother was going a little crazy.

"You must think I'm going crazy," Mom said, and now Jeep wondered if she had ESP too.

"Well, yeah, a little. It's like you're future Mom coming back to warn me that something bad is going to happen, but you can't tell me what it is because it would mess up the time continuum or something."

Mom laughed through her tears. "Oh, my bright girl. I'm so proud of you."

"You said that," Jeep smiled back gently. "So what's going to get me in trouble in the future that you remember somehow?"

"Yes," Mom said, remembering. "I'm so glad you have Blaine, he's such a good friend to you. And your other — oh, but I can't say more about that. It's what you need to know about the Traveler."

"The Buick."

"Yes, the Traveler that looks like an old Buick," the woman on the bed chuckled. "It's not that hard to operate, but you need at least to understand what it is."

"It's a car that you flew to Venus and Mars, and — where else?"

"That's the thing, dear, it's not just where, it's when, and both when and where combined."

"Try to start making sense for me, Mom."

"Right." Mom took a deep breath. "All right. It's not just about flying between planets, you see. The most important thing you need to know is that the Traveler goes through time and between — Oh!"

She held her hand to her temple, and then both hands to both temples, and said "Oh!" again.

"Mom? You OK?"

"Not now, not yet, no, no, no," Mom said, shaking her head between her palms. She looked up wildly into Jeep's eyes, suddenly in a frantic hurry to tell her daughter what she needed to know. "Gwin! The Traveler travels through space and time and —"

Then Mom cried a long, moaning cry that turned into more of a scream and made Jeep jump up and yell, "Help! Nurse!"

3

IN MOURNING

The funeral home smelled a little too sweet to be a house of death. And it was quiet — almost too quiet, like some stupid old movie full of ridiculous cliches.

And it made absolutely no sense to be sitting in an uncomfortable chair as people milled around and chuckled at the bulletin board full of old pictures of Mom. Jeep didn't know most of these people, although some of Mom's work colleagues were there and some kids from school. Most of them were people Dad and Mom must have known from a long time ago, or her work friends, so it was like being in a room full of strangers who wanted to tell her they knew how she felt.

Everything about the place felt artificial. What was that sweet smell, anyway? It was like some special air manufactured for funeral homes, some sort of chemically induced fresh air that sucked the sound out of the room. It was furnished like a living room from 30 years ago with couches and tables that looked brand new but hopelessly out of style.

And the urn on the table? Wrong, just wrong. That little

container of dust wasn't substantial enough to hold everything that Beverly Thompson was.

Jeep Thompson's mom was dead. There. It's said. She was sick for a long time, made it a little past her high school graduation, and started to tell her daughter the stuff she had been waiting for the right time to tell her, and died just before she told her the most important part.

Now it was time to say goodbye and all that, with the pomp and circumstance and the solemn looks and the "I'm so sorry for your loss," yeah, right. At least being cremated means no one was standing around and saying how peaceful her mom looked and all.

Something warm and fuzzy poked her hand, and she looked down to see a German shepherd with that wide-eyed, open-mouthed look dogs get that feels so much like a smile.

"Oh, Blaine," she said, kneeling and throwing her arms around the dog, which nuzzled her ear.

She held on until she heard a polite cough behind her.

"I'm very sorry, Ms. Thompson," the funeral director said with the sincere expression that funeral directors always have. "We don't allow animals except for service animals, and while I understand this is your friend ..."

"Sorry," said the dog, who quickly stood on his hind legs, grew less hairy and transformed into a tall young man with a droll expression who somehow managed also to be fully clothed. She once asked how he did that, and all he would say was, "Vampire trick."

Even here in the funeral home, Blaine looked like he was fighting to keep his mouth from turning up at the corners, and even though his face looked entirely sober, something about his eyes twinkled almost as if he wanted to say "How silly is this, a world where your mom is dead?"

What do you want from a vampire, anyway?

Jeep brushed hair out of her eyes and shrugged at Blaine.

"Thanks for coming," she said for the 43rd time that evening, meaning it for the first time. The big guy wrapped his arms around her and she felt safe. "I can't believe she's gone."

This won't do, this welling up of the eyes and the little break in her voice. Why wouldn't Blaine say something? He always has something droll to say. Instead he just sighed and squeezed a little harder, which made her eyes tear up even more, so she pushed him away.

Blaine blinked. "What?"

"I'm not in the mood for crying."

OK, now his face went full Blaine. That was more like it. His half-closed eyes and his little smile like he was seeing the whole world as his own private joke, and now Jeep Thompson knew the world was going to go on, just not for Mom. Mom —

"You are so in the mood for crying, G.P.," Blaine said. He was the only one who called her G.P. anymore. "Might as well get it over with."

"No, thank you very much, I'm trying to hold it together here," Jeep said. "Maybe later when it all seems more real than this. Right now I feel like I'm having some sort of ridiculous dream and I'm not allowed to wake up."

"Hmph," Blaine said. "Run with that."

"What, start running around the room screaming, 'Let me out! Let me out! I want to see my moth—'?" Jeep said, and her voice choked and her face scrunched up and she swayed on her feet and grabbed the front of Blaine's sweater and buried her scrunched-up face in his chest.

"That's better," he cooed, and maybe his voice sounded a little choked, too. "You need this, Jeep. I know."

Who was making that sound, Jeep thought? That muffled wailing sound like all of the hurtful things that ever happened had been bundled up in one place and discharged like some horrible siren against the cardigan. She realized it was her, of course, but a piece of her soul detached and felt the scene unfold with fascinated wonder: So this is how deeply she loved her mother, so much so that losing her unleashed a quivering, sobbing little girl from somewhere untapped since the beginning of time.

"There, there, dear, let it all out, you'll feel better," said a new, grandmotherly voice from somewhere behind her, and the spell was broken. Blaine was holding her as if she were made of gossamer, but somehow firmly enough that she felt safe, but Jeep stopped shaking, opened her eyes and looked to see who was trying to comfort her.

The woman wasn't all that old, maybe a little older than her mother, so almost 50, and she had a kind expression on her not-quite-wrinkled face with a twinkle in the green eyes behind rectangular eyeglasses.

"Are you all right?" the woman said. "Dear me, that's such a silly question, of course you're not." From somewhere she produced a tissue, and Jeep nodded and took the offering with a half-smile.

"I'll be OK," Jeep said. "I don't know where that came from."

"Oh, I do," the older woman said. "We all loved Beverly, and you're her daughter, after all. You loved her most of all."

The pain wanted to well back up and overflow again, but Jeep forced it down and nodded again, blowing her nose and using the tissue to its fullest use.

"I'm Diane Jacobus," the woman said, touching Jeep on the shoulder and looking her in the eyes. "Your mother and I go way back."

"I'm sorry, I don't know if she ever mentioned you."

Ms. Jacobus laughed. "No, of course not, dear, she wouldn't have been allowed to. We worked together on some very heady research."

4

THE MYSTERIOUS COLLEAGUE

Jeep's eyes widened, and even Blaine looked a little taken aback, and Jeep leaned forward and said in a loud whisper, "Oh my gosh, did you help build The Traveler?!"

Now it was the older woman's turn to widen her eyes, but she quickly narrowed them back to normal, looked both ways and over her shoulder, and said in a low voice, "Your mother should never have told you about that."

"Well," Blaine said drolly, because everything Blaine said came out droll, "the thing is sitting under a tarp in Jeep's garage, so it's not like some big classified secret."

"It's in your garage? Under a tarp? I was told top people were still working on it at an undisclosed location," Ms. Jacobus said, and then let out a little laugh. "Well, Bev is 'top people' if anyone is."

"But she hasn't touched it in years," Jeep said.

"No," the woman said, and seemed to be looking at something 1,000 miles away, "she wouldn't, not after losing Tom like that."

"Like what? I think she was going to tell me when she had the stroke," the younger woman said urgently. "What happened to my father?"

"This isn't the time to talk about it," Ms. Jacobus said, looking all around again. "Let's meet after the luncheon. You are having a luncheon, aren't you? It's my favorite part of funerals."

"Meet? Meet where?"

"How about in your garage? It would be so much easier to explain with the machine right there in front of us."

"I guess that makes as much sense as anything," Jeep said.

"Wait a minute," Blaine said. "How do we know you are who you say you are?"

Diane Jacobus looked down her nose through the eyeglasses as if she couldn't decide whether to be offended or amused.

"And you are —?"

"Blaine."

"Blaine who?"

"Blaine who wants to know if we can trust that you really used to work with Jeep's mother on the you-know-what."

"Blaine, behave," Jeep said reproachfully.

"I'm sorry, but something doesn't smell right about this," Blaine said, which gave Jeep pause. Being a vampire, Blaine's sense of smell was more attuned than regular people's.

"No, Blaine is absolutely right. The work was very important and very secret," Ms. Jacobus said, dropping her voice to a whisper with that last word. "Have you ever looked inside The Traveler, sat behind the steering wheel?"

Jeep looked at Blaine and back to Ms. Jacobus and back to Blaine and down at the floor. "Well, yeah. Yes, maybe I have, once or twice."

"Good," and she lowered her voice. "It's not round like a steering wheel, more like two butterfly wings attached to a round column, and there are three gauges in the dashboard marked 'Spatial,' 'Temporal' and 'Portal.' That's something you'd only know if you were familiar with the vehicle."

Jeep nodded.

"You could have broken into her garage and looked," Blaine said.

"Yes, I could have," Ms. Jacobus said. "But I didn't. I didn't even know it was there. I know what I know because I sat in the co-pilot seat and watched her mother fly the thing."

"What do they mean? The gauges," Jeep asked.

"Let's meet after the luncheon," The older woman repeated as people started to take seats in the gathering room and the funeral director solemnly approached them. "I'll share what I know then."

The service was very similar to almost every other funeral service, although Jeep had not been to enough funerals to know that for sure, but it was like her grandparents' funerals with the pastor and the readings and the people getting up to talk about what a special person Mom was and how she'll be missed. Truth be told, later on Jeep remembered laughing at all the right times and holding back tears most of the rest of the time, but she couldn't recall any of the specific things people said.

And the luncheon of chicken and stuffing and potatoes and vegetables and buttered rolls went by as these things do. Ms. Jacobus did seem to have a very good time, sitting at the same table at the pastor and laughing a great deal and having extra helpings of chicken and stuffing.

The number of times Jeep said "Thanks for coming" rose into the triple digits, and although it was comforting to know so many people came to her mother's funeral, her thoughts kept coming back to what Diane Jacobus might be able to tell her about the strange vehicle in the garage.

And what she had already said.

"We worked together on some very heady research ... Bev is 'top people,' after all ... not after losing Tom like that."

Not after losing Tom like that.

She knew how The Traveler worked. She had helped to build and operate it. She knew what happened to her father.

She knew what happened to her father.

"This isn't the time to talk about it."

But the time to talk about it was coming soon.

5

THE TRAVELER

Jeep and Blaine took the dusty old tarp off, which was more of a task than it sounds. The tarp was tied in the corners — more like lashed — and they needed to find a pair of scissors, then a sharp knife, before they could cut through the ropes that held the plastic covering to the vehicle.

Once they cleared that off, the gleaming black vehicle did resemble something off the highway from a long time ago.

"It really does kind of look like a 1965 Buick Riviera," Blaine said.

"I didn't know you knew anything about old cars," Jeep said.

Blaine smiled his droll smile. "I Googled it."

The covered headlamps, the bold contours of the vehicle, the tires and the windows very much resembled the sleek, solid tanks that mid-20th century Americans prowled the roadways in, but the wheel wells were hermetically sealed, the doors looked more like airplane hatches, and there were none of the visible seams one might see on a vehicle intended to stay on the ground and in atmosphere.

"This baby probably gets three miles to the gallon," Jeep said, running her hand over the massive front fender, and then she stopped and looked at her companion. "What do you think it runs on? Not gas."

"Rockets burn liquid nitrogen."

"Rocket boosters are 150 feet tall. There's no room in this thing for that kind of boost."

"Nuke? Some kind of renewable energy? How do you charge it? Where do you get fuel?"

Jeep shook her head, shifting her attention from the big machine to search the shelves on the garage wall. "It'd be too easy to find all that in a manual, or any of Mom's notes, I guess." There was no obvious binder full of papers, laptop that could be full of files, or even a significant-looking thumb drive or disc.

"Diane Jacobus could probably give you some of those answers."

"If she wants to tell us. The more I think about it, I think you were right to be leery of her, Blaine. Didn't you get the feeling she didn't really want to tell us anything about this machine?"

"Absolutely. She was like something out of an old spy movie. Maybe The Lady Vanishes."

"Huh?"

"I showed you that once. Really old movie, set in a train, sweet old coot disappears and turns out to be a covert operative."

"I think I remember it. It had a plucky heroine and her handsome dude sidekick."

He raised his eyebrows. "He was more than a sidekick, I believe, but I'd rather be the handsome dude sidekick than a paramour anyway."

"I'm glad," she said, looking at him askance. "We'd never be able to have a romantic meal together, with your uncooked meat and blood drinks. Eww."

"I'll never understand why you have to have the blood boiled out of everything, and you'll never understand why I need it raw," he said. "It's simple biology."

"I know," Jeep said. "I do understand, I just think it's a little icky."

On that point, they agreed to disagree and lapsed into a thoughtful silence while they waited for Diane Jacobus to arrive.

And waited.
And waited.
And waited.
And waited.

6

END OF WAITING

"She's not coming, is she?"

Blaine shook his head.

"It doesn't appear likely," he said.

It was now late afternoon, and Jeep and Blaine had been sitting in the garage for an hour and a half. "I'll be right behind you," Diane Jacobus had said. "You go on ahead. I have your address."

A half-hour after they took the tarp off, Jeep started to get antsy. After an hour she was a mixture of anxious and angry. Now 90 minutes had passed, and Jeep was starting not to believe in Diane Jacobus anymore.

The Thompson place was a little ways out of town along a side road. The house was modest compared to where a pair of astrophysicists might be expected to live, and it sat in a wooded area among five acres of land, which also included a fairly large field that couldn't be seen from the road. After Jeep had learned that The Traveler was some sort of spaceship, she started to think the field would make a good runway.

She had been expecting that Ms. Jacobus would be able to answer that question and many more — the most important question being "What happened to my father?" — and the woman's failure to appear was more than a little distressing.

"Was she just some scam artist or something?" Jeep said. "Or like you said, a spy, trying to find out where The Traveler was, and I steered her right to it?"

"That was a pretty accurate description of the dashboard, so she knows enough about the machine to be dangerous," Blaine said. "And by dangerous, I mean the spy thing. Is there anyone you know that you could call for help?"

She shook her head and peered through the driver's side window again. Instead of a back seat, The Traveler had some sort of electronic or pneumatic device behind the pilot and co-pilot chairs, and the dashboard consisted of an on/off switch, an altimeter and airspeed and attitude indicator, along with the three gauges that Ms. Jacobus had described.

"Spatial, Temporal, and Portal," Blaine mused. "What do you suppose they measure?"

"I guess 'spatial' has something to do with where you want to go in outer space," Jeep said, earning a near eye-roll from Blaine. "Well, if you figured it out already, why did you ask me what they mean?"

"It's the other two I was wondering about."

"Mom said it was a time machine, so 'Temporal' is probably where you want to go in time."

"Or when."

"Right. Could it be as simple as setting a time or date as your destination?"

"If that's the case, maybe we shouldn't touch it until we understand how it runs better."

Jeep nodded, and then she smiled a ginormous smile. "You want to take it out for a test drive, too, don't you, Blaine?"

"G.P., obviously you inherited this thing, so you should see what she's got," Blaine grinned. He opened a heavy door and climbed into the passenger seat. Jeep clambored behind the wheel.

"We probably should wait for Ms. Jacobus," she said.

"No, we shouldn't," he said, reaching behind to grab the shoulder harness and strap himself in. She returned the grin and strapped in.

"OK," she said, and pushed a button that said "Start." The dashboard lit up, and something started to hum behind them.

"Look at the Spatial gauge," Blaine said.

"No way," Jeep said.

The digital readout said "Venus." She adjusted the dial and found readouts for "Europe," "Asia," "India," "Chicago," "Portsmouth," and "Mars."

"Portsmouth?" Blaine said.

"MARS?" Jeep said, and turned it back to "Venus."

"Wait, maybe we should take a test drive around the block before we aim for other planets."

"Come on, man," she said. "Aim for the stars, right?"

He grinned a droll grin and sighed.

"JEEP? JEEP THOMPSON! ARE YOU IN THERE?"

They jumped at the amplified voice from somewhere outside the building. It sounded vaguely familiar in an authoritarian kind of way.

Jeep looked at Blaine sharply. "Is that —"

"JEEP, THIS IS DIANE JACOBUS. YOU NEED TO KNOW THAT YOU'RE SURROUNDED BY ARMED PERSONNEL. I KNOW YOU TURNED THE TRAVELER ON, AND YOU NEED TO TURN IT OFF RIGHT NOW AND COME OUT."

7

ESCAPE TO VENUS

"What in the wide, wide world of sports is this all about?" Blaine said.

"Ms. Jacobus must be some kind of cop," Jeep said.

"Or someone who wants to steal the tech," Blaine said, less encouragingly.

They looked at each other and said, simultaneously, "Let's get out of here."

Now, a moment ago it had occurred to Jeep to switch the switch back to somewhere closer to home. "Portsmouth" sounded especially homey, for some reason. Maybe Mom had mentioned that city sometime. But any thought of manipulating gauges had been sidetracked by the newcomers' arrival, and now her attention was further diverted by something crashing through the window of the garage, followed by a sudden sound along the lines of "WHUMP" and a flash that seemed to be something like, well, a flash bomb.

The young woman who was destined to save the worlds grinned and held her finger over the ignition switch.

"Ready, Blaine?"

"Ready as I'm ever going to be," drawled Blaine. "Punch it!"

"OK, here goes. I hope Mom knew what she was doing when she built this thing," she said, holding on to the wing-shaped steering wheel and flipping the switch.

"Wait," said Blaine. "What? What does that mean, 'I hope Mom knew what she was doing'?"

Everything began to vibrate.

"Next stop, Venus!" the girl cried.

"Are you sure about this, Jeep?" the vampire said.

"Of course not!" she shouted over the rumbling. "Who's ever sure about anything new? That's why you do it!"

Something pinged against a window.

"And then there's the little matter of those people shooting at us!" Jeep shouted. "Ready or not, here we go!"

And she punched it.

The machine burst through the garage door, and she aimed for the field. Light pressure on the accelerator sent them careening forward, and then went from zero to highway speed almost instantly. Alarmed men and women in suits and sunglasses dove out of the way, some of them firing weapons.

"Yikes! This thing goes a lot faster than I expected," she said. They quickly reached the edge of the clearing, and she pointed the machine down the length of the grassy field.

"STOP, JEEP! YOU DON'T KNOW HOW IT WORKS!" came an amplified voice from behind.

"She's got that right," she told Blaine, "but I don't like the idea of being shot or arrested or something."

"But it's set for Venus!" Blaine said, his calm voice perhaps a little higher-pitched than usual. "Shouldn't we aim for somewhere a little closer?"

"No time!" Jeep said. "I can probably adjust the direction once we're airborne." And as if to punctuate her words, several more pings pinged against the windows. "Gotta go!" she said and punched hard on the accelerator. "I hope we can clear the trees or this is a short trip."

Not only did the vehicle clear the trees, but it shot almost vertically into the sky, zipped through the troposphere, stratosphere, mesosphere, thermosphere and exosphere and left Earth's gravitational pull in the time it took her to say "or this is a short trip."

"Good newt!" Blaine shrieked. "Are you kidding me?"

As if watching a sped-up video of Earth taken from the International Space Station, they saw the planet disappear beneath and behind them, cruised past the moon some distance away, and plummeted into the dark void.

A bright spot in the distance appeared to grow to the size of a coin, then a green beach ball, and soon it became clear they were already approaching another celestial body.

"Is that what I think it is?" Jeep shouted.

"If you think it's Venus, I have to say I think you're right," Blaine shrieked. She wasn't used to the sound of Blaine shrieking.

"We've only been flying about three minutes," she said. "How is that possible?"

"I have no idea," Blaine said, a little less shrieky, "but that's a planet, and it's not Earth, and we aimed for Venus, so do the math."

She pulled back on the throttle-thing, and the rumbling drew back to a more manageable and somewhat pleasant vibration. The huge green orb ahead grew at a more reasonable pace, and they began to believe they would have a chance to land there rather than splat against it.

"It's beautiful, isn't it?" Jeep said.

"You don't need my permission to think so," Blaine sniffed.

"Say, on the dark side of the planet," Jeep said. "Are those lights? like the lights of cities?"

Blaine peered into the darkness.

"They're lights," he acknowledged. "I'd have to be closer to know if they're cities."

"But they could be."

"Have you ever been to Venus? Neither have I," he sniffed. "I don't have a clue what causes light during the night on Venus, and I've never heard of cities up here."

"But they look like the light of Earth cities."

"As you like to say, my dear: Duh."

"That's all I'm saying!" Jeep said.

"So: Venus inhabited?" Blaine raised his pointed eyebrows.

"Not in any universe I ever knew about!" she cried. It's amazing how prescient that particular statement turned out to be.

"So: Shall we land on the day side or the night side?" Blaine asked. "I vote day."

"Makes sense. How do you suppose you land this thing?"

"Oh, dear. You made taking off look so easy, I just thought you knew how to land."

Jeep peered at the controls.

"If this thing flies like an airplane, I may have a fighting chance of getting us down," she said. "Assuming a real airplane reacts like a video-game airplane."

"Oh, my," Blaine sighed. "How did we get into this?"

"How hard could it be?" Jeep said.

Blaine, who normally was unflappable, had been beginning to show signs of flapping, but now he looked out the window, took several deep breaths, turned back to his human friend, and smiled a droll grin.

"You got this, G.P.," he said, only a trace of a tremor in his voice. "Go for it."

She smiled back and peered out the windshield. Taking her cues from the video-game simulator back home, Jeep gently pushed the steering wheel forward, and The Traveler began to descend.

There were a few anxious moments when the Buick glowed and was surrounded by what appeared to be flames, and it grew warmer inside of the vehicle, but a moment later the conflagration subsided and they were descending through a relatively normal-looking sky. They burst through cloud cover and were surprised to see landscapes that looked almost earthly in a Venusian kind of way.

"Are those forests down there? Isn't Venus a lifeless rock?" Jeep said.

"Something like that," Blaine said. "Although I always heard it was sort of steamy."

"This looks almost normal," she said. "Some of the colors seem off. Whoa!" she added, pointing to a cluster that looked suspiciously like a small town. "Is that a —"

"— small town? I think so!"

"What is going on?!"

"I don't know, but maybe we should land somewhere away from civilization, or whatever that is," Blaine offered.

"Right. Does that look like an open field, over there to the left, down there?" she said, pointing.

"Open-ish," Blaine said. "Give it a shot."

Jeep hesitated. "I sure wish we had found the manual."

"How do you do when you land with your video game simulator?" Blaine said.

"Most of the time I just turn it off without landing," she admitted.

"How do you do with landing?" he repeated.

"Not so good," Jeep said. "But how hard could it be?"

Blaine shrieked.

8

UNEXPECTED HELP

"It appears you are trying to land," a digital voice barked suddenly from somewhere, as The Traveler dropped to about 2,000 feet above the surface of Venus. "Would you like to initiate landing sequence?"

Jeep Thompson looked across the cabin to Blaine in the co-pilot seat. He shrugged.

"No way," she said. "It couldn't be that easy, could it?"

"Landing sequence aborted," the voice said.

"What?!" It was Jeep's turn to shriek.

"You said 'No way,'" Blaine said.

"What?!?!"

"It asked if you wanted to initiate the landing sequence, and you said, 'No way.'"

"Oh, no. I mean yes. Yes! Yes! Landing sequence!"

"Would you like to initiate landing sequence?" the voice said again.

"Yes! Please! Absolutely! Yes! Yes!"

"Initiating landing sequence."

They both sighed audibly. The steering wheel began to move on its own, and Jeep relinquished control.

As the vehicle glided over the landscape, they had a chance to look at the scenery more closely. A vast forest sprawled below, except for the large clearing that grew closer and closer as they descended.

"It looks like a forest," Blaine said. "I mean, an Earth forest. Green. I would have expected different colors than ours."

"I suppose chlorophyll is chlorophyll, so the trees would be green anywhere," Jeep said.

"If we're going to land on another planet, I wish it would look like another planet."

"I'm sure we'll notice some differences up close," she said, "assuming we survive the landing."

Blaine raised his eyebrows. "You are one of the most optimistic people I know, most of the time. What happened?"

"My mother died, I got shot at, and we flew to Venus in five minutes," Jeep said. "It all tends to disturb your equilibrium."

The Traveler bounced on a cushion of air turbulence.

"I see your point," Blaine said. "Well," he added, as the forest broke and suddenly the wide clearing was all around them, "we'll know whether we're going to survive in three — two —"

The vehicle's tires struck the surface roughly and they bounced a little higher than would be comfortable in an earthly landing, but since it was Venus and they were relieved they did not splat, they said "Whoa!" in unison and braced for a second impact, which turned out to be somewhat gentler.

They rolled over rough but not rugged ground, kicking up dust and divots as The Traveler sped through high grass, and a quiet but efficient brake of some sort pushed them against their safety harnesses as the machine decelerated quickly. After a few rambunctiously bouncy moments, the vehicle rolled to a halt.

They heard a faint hissing sound that stopped after a few seconds, and the digital voice said, "Landing sequence completed."

The young woman and the vampire exhaled and made eye contact.

"Holy crap," Jeep Thompson said. "We're on Venus."

"You're welcome," the digital voice said.

9

THE CLEARING

They were near the edge of the clearing and could now see that the trees towered overhead. They slowly opened the doors and stepped into the light.

A light breeze was breezing, and the air was warm and thick.

"Wow, it's muggy," Blaine said. "We might be overdressed."

"Do you hear what I hear?" Jeep said.

It seemed like a loaded question. There was a lot to hear. The trees, which resembled Earth trees except their leaves were all wrong, were rustling in the breeze. A horde of some sort of cricket-like creatures was singing cricket-like songs all around them. Birds, which looked almost exactly like any birds but didn't quite, were chirping and calling and tweeting away up above; some were even flying about now that the ruckus of the Traveler landing had ended.

But that wasn't what Jeep heard. Far off in the distance was the sound of something that was not a breeze or an insect or a bird. It was a whine or a rumble or a dull roaring of machines along ...

"Is that —" Blaine began.

"It sounds like a highway!"

"... or at least a country road," he offered.

"So here is a forest of trees with leaves that don't look like any trees we've ever seen, crickets that don't exactly sound like crickets except they do, and birds with markings that don't match anything on Earth," Jeep said, "so it stands to reason, why wouldn't there be people who don't quite look like Earthlings driving machines that don't quite look like our cars and trucks?"

"And the reason people have never seen anything like this on the surface of Venus is —"

"I don't know. Maybe they didn't look hard enough, or they didn't look in the right places," she said. "Maybe all those clouds people saw in their telescopes were some sort of screen the Venusians put up to keep us from seeing what's really down here."

Blaine thought for a moment. "Anything's possible when you think of it."

"Do we want to walk toward that road noise and leave the Traveler here, or do we want to drive the Traveler out to the road?" she said.

Blaine assessed the thick forest around the clearing. "I don't think there's a road to the road."

"We could fly over it."

"What if they don't have flying cars and we freak them out?"

"Good point," she said. "Let's leave the Traveler here and walk a little way to see how far it is to the road."

"Is it safe to leave the Traveler?" he asked tentatively. "It's our only way to get home."

"You'd think there must be a way to lock it. I bet there's a key."

They clambored back into the vehicle and started looking in nooks and crannies and pockets and compartments, but no key presented itself.

"Huh," Jeep said. "How do you secure this thing?"

"Would you like to initiate lockup mode?" the Traveler's voice said.

They looked at each other.

"That makes too much sense," Blaine said with his wry smile.

"Wait," Jeep said. "OK, Traveler, how do we unlock you when we get back?"

"Help mode," it said, paused a moment and added, "To initiate unlock mode, say, "Initiate unlock mode.""

"Just ask?"

"Correct."

"So anyone can just say, 'Initiate unlock mode,' and it unlocks?" Blaine said a bit skeptically.

"Incorrect. Commands respond only to the commander or passenger."

"Come on, we just met this afternoon. How do you know who we are?" Jeep said.

"You just flew to Venus. Therefore you are the commander."

"There's a logic to that, kind of, sort of," Blaine admitted.

"All right, we either trust the thing to work or we stay within eyesight," she said. "OK, Traveler, initiate lockup mode."

"Initiating lockup mode."

They got out of the vehicle and closed the doors, which emitted an extra hiss and a decided CHUNK sound. Heretofore invisible panels slid over the door handles and effectively sealed the vehicle from entry.

"Cool," Jeep said.

They turned in the direction of the highway-like noises and walked into the forest.

10

FAMILIAR BUT NOT

As it happened, the road was not as far off as they expected.

There was plenty of room between the trees to walk, although there was not enough room to drive a vehicle the size of the Traveler between them. Up ahead they could see occasional movement, like glimpses of vehicles flashing by, and it wasn't long before they could see a very Earth-like road surface through the brush.

Being new to the neighborhood, they paused rather than rush out and stand by the road to see what kind of creature would drive what kind of vehicle up to them.

"Well, there's a road," Jeep said. "I wonder where it goes?"

"If it's like our roads, anywhere you want to go," Blaine said. "Drive down the road in front of your house and you can be three states away by nightfall, if you want."

"Do you think the Traveler would blend in with other cars and we could go for a ride, look around?"

"Let's see what drives by."

At that, they could hear something approaching. A few moments later they got a glimpse of a silver vehicle of some sort.

The extent to which it resembled your basic Earth sedan was somewhat unnerving. It appeared to have four wheels — the glimpse was too glimpsey to say whether they were rubber tires — a windshield, and doors where an Earthling might expect to find doors. Light from the sun glanced off the windows, so it was impossible to tell what kind of person or creature might be inside.

Blaine tsked.

"You would think if we went to Venus, the cars at least would not look like every other car on the road," he said drily. "That could have been a Buick or a Toyota."

"Well, that's good, isn't it? It means we could drive on their roads if we wanted. The Traveler doesn't look that much different, does it?"

"I suppose if you want to travel by ground and you're not in a hurry, we could drive it like a car," Blaine said. "Why are there roads and city lights on Venus?"

The question was so sudden and so logical that Jeep was caught up short.

"There are city lights because there are cities here, I suppose," she said with a grin. "And you need roads to get between cities."

Another car swished by. This one was blue and, again, indistinguishable from an Earth vehicle.

"So weird," Blaine said under his breath.

"The car or what I said?" the red-haired girl said, green eyes flashing in the Venusian sun.

"Both," he chuckled. "Aren't you the least bit curious why Venus is so much like Earth when every spacecraft people have sent here has found hot desolation?"

"I am a lot more than the least bit curious. In fact, I'm extremely curious," she said, and brought the palm of her hand to the back of her neck. "At least they got the 'hot' part right."

Blaine fingered the leaves on a small tree. They were almost perfectly triangular.

"It's like Earth, only hotter and with everything just a little bit off," he said.

"Well, the flora and fauna are going to need to live in a different atmosphere, so they're going to adapt differently as they evolve," Jeep said. "It's kind of bizarre that the cars look so much like ours. There are other ways to design a vehicle."

Blaine snorted. "Got that right."

Another vehicle was coming, and they could tell this one was different. For one thing, the ground rumbled as it approached. As it came into sight, they saw it was a big, black truck-like thing with six wheels. It had an enclosed cab and a long bed in the back, like a pickup truck or — since a half-dozen humanoids wearing armor and helmets were sitting in the back — a troop carrier.

"Well, they have armies here, or police," Blaine said.

"Let's get back to the Traveler and take it somewhere."

A red squirrel chittered at them from halfway up a 12-foot tree nearby.

"Hel-lo," Jeep said with great interest. It looked like a terran squirrel but, of course, not exactly. The red fur was redder than fur tends to get on Earth, almost hunter orange, and its ears were pointed with little tufts of hair reaching for the sky. "He's cute."

"Hmph," Blaine said. "I hope we don't have to kill the wildlife to get a meal."

"Blaine!" She was shocked.

"Don't worry," he said. "I'm not hungry. Yet."

They wandered back in silence, looking around at the lush forest that looked like every forest and no forest they'd ever seen.

So immersed in exploration were they that when they reached the clearing and saw the Traveler out in the grass, they pulled up short.

There, standing between them and the vehicle, was the largest human being either had ever seen.

The man towered over the two travelers. He wasn't big and fat so much as simply huge. His mass didn't jiggle like a jolly fat man, it just stood there, solid, imposing and more than a little intimidating. As if that wasn't enough, he held some sort of cane or stick in his hands, a long, thick rod that was rounded at both ends, that perhaps could be construed as a weapon.

Blaine took a step back; Jeep just looked up and said, "Hey. I'm Jeep, this is Blaine."

The huge man looked down at the two adventurers and said, "Gentle. Bill Gentle. My friends call me Little Bill. They think it's cute."

"What do you think?" Jeep said.

"I think you're trespassing," said Little Bill Gentle.

11

FIRST CONTACT

Bill Gentle had a big square face that on a smaller man might look friendly and reassuring, but its bigness felt a little threatening.

"How'd you get your car in the middle of my field?" he asked. "That path you carved through the grass, it almost looks like you flew in and coasted to a stop, but this thing doesn't have wings."

Jeep and Blaine looked at each other.

"Their aircraft have wings?" she muttered. "Another thing just like Earth."

"What did you just say to him?" Bill said. "We're talking here, you two and me, I wanna hear what you're saying."

"Sorry," Jeep said. "We're not from around here. We got lost and touched down in your field. Sorry."

"Huh. So it does fly," the big man said, setting one end of the stick on the ground so it looked more like a cane than a club. "How do you get it off the ground?"

"I don't know," she said. "It was my mom's. She knows how it works, but —"

"She's dead," Blaine said. "She just died the other day." Jeep wondered why Blaine would divulge that bit of information. This guy didn't need to know her life story.

"That's too bad," the big man said, and his expression softened. "Kid your age is too young not to have a mother around."

"Yeah, well —" Jeep began, but her voice trailed off.

"Can't get sentimental," Little Bill said, almost to himself, and then set his shoulders and jaw. "You're on my land, and you need to move along. I've half a mind to call the constabulary, except they're so busy."

"No need for that," Blaine said. "We're sorry. We'll be on our way."

"Where are you going?"

Now that was a very good question.

"Well, we're just flying around looking at scenery," Jeep said. "Do you —"

"Why are they so busy?" Blaine asked.

"Huh?" Jeep and Bill said in unison.

"The — constabulary. You said they're so busy."

Little Bill Gentle looked at him sideways. "How do I know you're not from the Castle? I don't want any trouble around here."

"I didn't even know there was a Castle until you mentioned it," Jeep said. "So you have a king or queen or some sort of royalty?"

"Some sort of royalty, yeah. I guess you aren't from around here after all. Unless you have something to do with it."

"With what?" Jeep asked.

He looked her in the eye, seemed to come to a conclusion, and sighed.

"The Prince is missing."

"The Prince —?"

"Prince Viktar. He drove off and hasn't been seen since."

"How long ago is this?"

"A few days. The family has a summer place not far from here, and they thought maybe he would come out this way, but he hasn't arrived."

"Is that why you checked your field?" Blaine asked. "In case he —"

"Nah, I walk the land every day. I need the exercise," Bill said. "Most days it's just a nice walk, but every so often I see something that needs fixing," his eyes narrowing.

"Well, no, we didn't even know who Prince Viktar is," Jeep admitted. "But we'll be on our way."

If Bill had not already narrowed his eyes, he would narrow them now. "Right. You said you aren't from around here. Where is it that you're from, exactly?"

"Well —"

"You probably wouldn't believe us," Blaine interjected. Jeep glanced at him sharply. What was he doing?

"I don't know," the big man said. "I believe a lot of stuff."

"My friend just means you don't seem to trust us," she said, pushing Blaine toward his side of the Traveler. "We'll get going."

"Now, hang on just a little bit," Bill said. "How do I know for sure you're not part of some group that kidnapped the Prince and I should be thinking about turning you in?"

"You don't want to do that," Jeep said.

"No, I don't. I just want to know where you're from and what you're really doing in my field."

"Well, we're from pretty far away from here, and I don't pay attention to politics, that's why we didn't know about the Prince," she said, trying to figure out how to explain where they lived when she didn't know any Venusian place names.

"We're from Earth," Blaine blurted. "This is our spaceship."

Jeep whirled to look at Blaine. What was he doing?!

Bill stared at the two of them, then smiled.

"Well, that's not around here at all," he said, then turned darker. "Why are you fooling with me? You seem like good kids, for trespassers. Are you running from something? Come on, maybe I can help."

No, you can't help, unless you can explain why a nice old lady with a small army back on Earth wants to take her mother's space machine away and was willing to shoot the two of them, Jeep thought.

"I don't think you can help us, but thanks," she said. "Blaine, come on —"

"Maybe you can help," Blaine said. "We're kind of lost."

This time she turned to him and said it out loud: "Blaine. What. Are. You. DOING?"

Bill put his arm out, palms up, and continued to smile. "OK, then. Start with where you are really from? I know nobody is from Earth, so what? Are you from Argossie? I could understand your not knowing who Prince Viktar is if you're from Argossie."

"What do you mean, you know nobody is from Earth?" Jeep said. "I'm not saying that's where we're from —" nudging Blaine in the ribs "— but it's not impossible."

"Come on, they've sent space probes out there," Bill said. "There's nothing there. It's kind of pretty, but it's empty."

"Earth has sent space probes to Venus, and they found a big rock," Blaine said. "Our own space probes say you don't exist." And in response to another wild look from Jeep, he added, "Come on, our first contact with alien life and we're not going to be straight with them? We're not politicians; let's just be honest."

"Who you calling an alien there, little feller?" Bill said, sounding a bit miffed.

"Blaine didn't mean it personally, Mr. Gentle," Jeep said. "You have to admit we seem a little different from each other, and —" conceding the point "— we're not even from the same planet."

Bill Gentle stood before them looking more befuddled by the moment.

"So you're sticking with the monsters from Earth story, then," he said. "I'd have to say it's even more understandable that you wouldn't know the prince, but give me a break here, you have to admit it's pretty far-fetched."

"We, um, come in peace and all. We really just want to take a look around," Jeep said.

"Although we left behind some people who weren't very peaceful," Blaine added.

"So were you running from somebody or just flying around looking at the scenery?" Bill said. "You two really need to get your stories straight."

"It's a little bit of both," Jeep conceded. "We wanted to try out Mom's Traveler and some thugs showed up and kind of forced the issue."

"The Traveler? That's what you call this?" the big man turned his attention to the vehicle. "Why does that name sound familiar?"

"CITIZENS!"

The new voice came from the edge of the clearing and was spoken in the universal tone of authority.

12

CASTLE GUARD

For a nanosecond Jeep thought Diane Jacobus' gunmen had found them.

The three of them turned and saw a couple of uniformed people in helmets walking toward them. It looked like the same attire the folks on the troop-carrier-type vehicle had been wearing. There was a tall, muscular male soldier and a compact female one who also seemed buff.

"It's the Castle Guard. You better be nice to them," Bill Gentle whimpered.

"Great," Blaine muttered.

"Hello!" Jeep said, raising her hand.

"PUT YOUR HAND DOWN. STAND RIGHT THERE," the compact soldier said. "DON'T MOVE."

The newcomers strode over the grass and planted themselves not far from our trio. The female soldier touched a button on her bicep that appeared to shut off an amplifier of some sort.

"What are you doing here?" the woman barked.

"I'm taking a walk in my field," Little Bill Gentle said meekly. "My friends here were —"

"What kind of vehicle is this? How did it get here?"

"It's called The —" Jeep began.

"What have you done with Prince Viktar?" the taller soldier said sharply.

"If you'd let us explain —" Blaine said.

"I think we'll sort this out at the base," the compact soldier said. "We're taking you into custody."

"OK," Bill said.

"What? Why?" Jeep spluttered.

"Suspicion of abducting the prince," she said as if it was a dumb question. "Why else would you be out here 'taking a walk' in the middle of nowhere?"

"Let's get out of here," Jeep said. "Initiate unlock mode!"

"Initiating unlock mode," The Traveler said.

"What are you doing?" the female soldier said. "Stay where you are!"

"We should take Bill with us," Jeep murmured. "How do we fit him in The Traveler?"

"Do you need more passenger space?" The Traveler said.

"What? Yes!" Jeep cried.

There came a whirring sound, and the machine stretched itself out, revealing a second set of doors and a back seat.

"How did you do that?" Bill Gentle said.

"I don't know," Jeep said. "Get in!"

"I'm not sure about this —" Bill said.

"Don't go any further!" the larger soldier barked. Blaine ran up to Bill, opened the back door, and pushed the big man in, then jumped in the front passenger seat. Jeep was already fastening her seat belt and punched the Start button.

"CITIZENS! HALT!"

"Are you crazy?" Bill called from behind them. Everyone jerked as The Traveler started rolling.

The two soldiers waved their arms, running next to the vehicle until it pulled away. Jeep accelerated as fast as the machine would allow and lifted into the sky.

"Whoa!" Bill Gentle said, staring at the disappearing ground and then at the two strangers in the front seat. "What have you done?! They're going to hunt us down now."

"I don't feel like getting arrested today," Jeep called back. "It sounded like they were going to railroad us for kidnapping the prince."

"You DID kidnap the prince?"

"No! Of course not! We never heard of him until five minutes ago," she said. "But they didn't seem to care."

"What do we do now, though?" Blaine said. "We probably got Bill in trouble, so we can't go back to Earth, and we can't just drop him off somewhere because they'll be after him now, too."

"I guess we're going to have to find the prince," Jeep said.

"Find somebody we never heard of until five minutes ago, while the Castle Guard chases us on suspicion of kidnapping?" Blaine said skeptically.

"Best idea I've got. Any alternatives?"

"We should give ourselves up," Bill said. "They'll give us a shorter sentence if we decide to cooperate."

"They wouldn't even let us finish a sentence! They're not interested in cooperation, they just want their prince back. So we'll find him ... somehow ..."

13

LAY OF THE LAND

Little Bill Gentle was a docile man for such a big guy, and he certainly seemed terrified of this Castle Guard.

"I guess I know why you ran, but you've really put us in a mess," he had told Jeep and Blaine as they rummaged through his kitchen. They gathered provisions as fast as they could, knowing the authorities would quickly figure out who Bill was (seeing as he'd made a comment about "my field," so they could determine who owned the field and where his home was) and could be there at any moment.

Bill Gentle explained that the Castle Guard worked for the royal family and basically ruled over the citizenry, and Prince Viktar was the boss, he explained to his new Earthling acquaintances. (The Traveler being unlike any Venusian technology, he was getting used to the idea that Jeep and Blaine came from somewhere else.) Viktar was not the most ruthless of rulers — that would be his sister Precipice — but he wasn't the nicest fellow, either, and so the populace lived in general fear of their Guard.

Precipice was leading the family and therefore the government with Viktar missing, and she would take the throne if he were to turn up dead. Bill explained these facts as if it would be a pretty miserable princedom if Precipice were the ultimate authority.

"What do you call this place, anyway?" Blaine asked. "Does it have a name?"

"I keep forgetting you're not from around here," Bill said after staring at him for a few moments. "The principality is known as Zeldelae, and this town is called Gustovia."

"This wooded area is in a town?"

"Downtown Gustovia is about 5 rollocks that way," he said, pointing. "Towns claim all of the surrounding area as their territory."

"Right, we have a system like that, too," Blaine nodded.

"Zeldelae is one of a half-dozen countries on this continent," Bill said.

"Argossie must be very far away, since you thought that's the only reason we wouldn't know about Prince Viktar," Jeep said.

"Right. I'd better bring my bongrik," the big man said, lifting the long rod he had been carrying when they met.

"What's a bongrik?" Jeep asked, curious.

"It's that big stick," Blaine stated the obvious.

Bill lifted the stick almost reverantly. "The bongrik is an elegant weapon for a more civilized age," he said softly, almost whispering.

Blaine rolled his eyes. "Where have we heard THAT before?"

Suddenly the stick was whirling in Bill Gentle's hands. He spun around and halted the weapon millimeters from the side of Blaine's head.

"Mock the bongrik at your peril," Bill hissed.

Blaine glanced sideways at the end of the stick and dissolved into fog.

"What the —" said Bill Gentle, but then a vicious looking dog emerged from the fog and wrapped his teeth around the stick, with the big man holding on fast.

"Blaine's a vampire," Jeep said.

"Ain't no such thing," Bill said, and dipped his wrist suddenly, which caused the stick to fling the dog high into the air. Snarling, the canine dissipated into fog, and Jeep's droll friend materialized in front of them.

"Mock vampires at your own peril," Blaine said calmly.

The two of them stared at each other for a moment, and then Bill set the bongrik down, holding it like a walking stick.

"Well, you definitely aren't from around here."

"OK, guys, I honestly think we're on the same side here," Jeep said, stepping between them.

"Believe it or not, I tend to agree," said Bill Gentle. "We ought to get going."

"Do you have any idea where the prince might be?" Jeep said.

"He's not here," said the large man. "But the Castle Guard is coming anyway, thanks to you two."

"You don't have to help us," Jeep said. "We're really sorry. You can tell them we made you come along."

"That much was obvious, I think," Bill said. "But they won't be nice to me anyway. We'd better go."

And so, loaded with provisions and Bill's bongrik and not much of an idea where to go next, the unlikely threesome lifted over the trees.

"You said the prince's family has a summer place near here," Blaine said. "Should we try there first?"

"I don't know if that's such a great plan," said Jeep as she tried to stick as close to the top of the wooded canopy as she could. "The place is probably crawling with cops."

"What's a cop?" Bill asked.

"Something like your Castle Guard, only maybe a little nicer."

"Sometimes," Blaine said a tad ruefully. "They do tend to pick on vampires."

"Do we know for sure that he was kidnapped?" Jeep asked. "Where would a prince go if he didn't want to be found?"

"Or, for that matter, where would kidnappers take a prince if they didn't want to be found?" Blaine said.

Bill Gentle looked thoughtful. "So there's a swamp about 10 rollocks that way," he said, pointing toward a darker green area in the distance. "There are some abandoned houses off the beaten track."

"Something the prince might secretly fix up and move in?" Blaine asked.

Bill shook his head. "Someplace kidnappers might take a prince where they didn't want to be found."

"Do many people know about these old houses?" Jeep asked.

"Sure, everybody does," Bill said. "People still don't go to the swamp, though. There's wildlife."

"Lions and tigers and bears," Blaine said. "Oh my."

"What's a bear?" Bill asked.

All of a sudden there was a bear where Blaine had been standing. A big, brown, furry bear with a droll expression on his face. He growled and raised his hand to say "hi," but even a friendly bear with a droll expression can look menacing.

"Oh!" Bill said, and with a sudden fierce expression on his face, he whipped out the big stick and began spinning it so fast it looked like a helicopter rotor.

The big man stopped its spin by grabbing the bongrik in both hands and bracing to swing it hard against the bear, but before he could follow through with what surely would be a devastating blow, Blaine the bear switched back to his human form.

"Oh!" Bill said again. "Is that what a vampire looks like?"

"No," Blaine said. "A vampire is a shape-shifter. A bear is the animal I just shifted into. That's what a bear looks like."

"Scary!"

"Not as scary as that stick."

"I told you. It's a bongrik."

"You have lions and tigers?" Jeep asked.

"Huh?" Bill and Blaine said in unison.

"Blaine said, 'Lions and tigers and bears, oh my,' and you said, 'What's a bear,' as if you knew what lions and tigers are," Jeep said.

"Oh, yes, yes, I do," Bill said.

"Venus has lions and tigers?" Blaine asked.

"Not around here. But the swamp is full of snoggles."

Blaine snorted. He couldn't help it. "Oh, no, not snoggles!" he groaned in delight. "Why did it have to be snoggles?"

"Laugh as much as you like, young man," Bill said. "You don't want to cross a snoggle."

Jeep and Blaine looked at each other and burst out laughing. Of course, they had never seen a snoggle and were judging a beast by its absurd name.

"We'll check out Snoggle Swamp," Jeep said, gliding in that direction. "I promise, we'll be careful." But her promise ended in a helpless giggle.

14

MISHAP IN SNOGGLE SWAMP

The sun was setting on the horizon as Jeep nestled the Traveler down onto a relatively dry patch of what she had named Snoggle Swamp.

It looked like any swamp among a thousand wetlands on Earth. High grass and cattails covered the area where they landed, and weeping trees and steam hung over the water at the edge of the clearing. It was hot and wet, of course, because swamps on Venus are always hot and wet. If you were closer to the sun by 26 million miles, you would be hot and wet all the time, too.

"So tell us about snoggles," Blaine said. "What do they look like? We ought to know what we're trying to avoid."

"Well, they have big round eyes that look like they glow in the dark, and a long nose that kind of hangs down in front of their mouth," Bill said. "They won't bother you unless you bother them, and even then they're slow to anger — they're never the first to attempt violence. Actually, I was going to say they're never the first to strike, but that's not quite accurate."

"So sometimes they do strike first?" Jeep said.

"No, because no living being has ever managed to strike first against a snoggle," the giant man said. "Not that people haven't tried. I would say snoggles are deceptively fast, but there's nothing deceptive about them. They're just so fast, faster than the eye can see, most of the time. If you try to hurt one, it'll hurt you back before you have a chance."

"Yikes. Sounds scary."

"Yes and no," Bill said. "Snoggles aren't violent unless they have to be. They believe in a fair fight, and it's not fair for snoggles to fight at all, because they're so much faster than anything else. But they'll keep you from starting a fight if it looks like you're going to."

"OK," Jeep said, walking through the grass. "So we just have to avoid making any aggressive moves."

"That's a good start," Bill agreed.

"'We come in peace,'" Blaine intoned.

"You don't want to disturb a sleeping snoggle, though," Bill said. "Because —"

Just then, Jeep stepped on a foot. She didn't do this deliberately. The foot was there in her path, and her own foot was on a certain trajectory, and, well, there you are.

And "it" happened to be a snoggle's foot. Now, it seems few howls are howlier than a snoggle howl. You may find, in the Venusian equivalent of a dictionary, a definition of the word howl that includes an illustration of a snoggle. The people of Earth have an expression: "She howled like a banshee." The closest translation into Venusian is, "She howled like a snoggle."

For what it's worth, this snoggle was a male, so the correct phrase would be "he howled like a snoggle," but to the common ear one snoggle's howl was like another. It was loud, and it was howly.

A wide-eyed creature jumped out of the grass holding its foot. Its droopy nose swung from side to side as it hopped and howled.

"Oh my goodness," Jeep said. "I'm so sorry."

"Owwwwww," the snoggle shouted. "You stepped on my foot!

What in the four empires of Zeldelae did you do that for? Owwwwww!"

"I may have mentioned that snoggles tend to whine," Bill said, holding his bongrik with both hands just in case. "I apologize if I didn't."

"Oh yeah, ya big galoot? It's easy not to whine when it's not your foot that got stepped on! Owwwwwww!"

"Good point," Bill conceded.

"And put that down, I'm not going to hurt you — not like she hurt me. Owwwwww!"

"Look, she said she was sorry —" Blaine said.

"But it still hurrrrrts, doesn't it?" the snoggle shrieked.

"This is quite a commotion. Did I break your foot?" Jeep asked, genuinely concerned.

The snoggle stopped howling and peered at the horizon, apparently testing to see if his foot hurt like it had been stepped on or if his foot hurt like it was broken.

"You know," he admitted after a few seconds, "no, it's not broken." Then, as if realizing he had stopped howling like a snoggle, he added, "But it still hurrrrrts!!"

"I'm so sorry," Jeep said again, and shot a warning glance at Blaine before he could say — as she instinctively knew he would — "Then it's no big deal," because obviously it was a big deal to this snoggle.

"This is odd," Bill said. "We should be dead."

"Why?!" asked Blaine.

"I was just getting to that. I've always heard that if you disturb a sleeping snoggle, it will rip off your head and the heads of everyone you're with, quick as you can."

"Well, you shouldn't believe everything you hear," said the snoggle. "But I do find this disturbing."

"And I did say I'm sorry, straight away, several times," Jeep said. "How can I make it better?"

"You can't," the snoggle said. "It still hurts. But I accept your apology."

"I appreciate that."

"But what did you do that forrrr?" the snoggle howled.

"I didn't see you there. It was an accident."

"Well, you should watch where you're going!" he snapped, drawing his long nose closer to hers.

"Yes, I should," Jeep said, backing her head away, and repeated, "I'm sorry."

"Hey, Snogger, keep it down over there," came a voice across the glen. They looked and saw two more round eyes shining in the growing darkness, and then two more a short distance away, and then two — no, four — more shining eyes, side by side, a little closer by.

"I have a bad feeling about this," Blaine said.

"Snoggles don't bother you unless you disturb them," Bill said.

"I don't know, I'm feeling pretty disturbed about now," one of the sets of eyes said — fortunately, the farthest one away.

"It's all right, everybody," said the snoggle named Snooger. "I'll deal with this."

15

INTERROGATION

Taking a closer look, they saw that their new acquaintance was a biped with a shaggy body and four clawed fingers and toes on its hands and feet. In addition to big round eyes and the dangly nose, it had round ears near the top of its head, something like a teddy bear crossed with an elephant, except his nose was wider than an elephant's trunk. Calling the ears "teddy bear ears" would be spot on, though.

"What are you doing in the swamp anyway?" Snooger asked. "It's not like there's any legitimate reason to be here at this time of night."

Jeep stepped forward and said, "We're looking for Prince Viktar."

If the wide, round eyes could get any wider, they did now. Snooger, the snoggle, burst into laughter and turned toward the others.

"Guys, guys, you gotta hear this," he chortled. "They're looking for Prince Viktar!"

The swamp rang with peals of laughter, chuckles, hoots, snorts and guffaws, except for one voice that said, "Still trying to sleep here."

Snooger looked over the three visitors with a snoggly grin.

"He's not here," he said. "But then if the prince didn't want to be found, he probably would ask his friends not to say where he is."

"Are you friends with the prince?" Blaine asked.

"That depends," said Snooger. "Are you?"

"Well —"

"Wrong answer. Nope. I don't know where the prince is."

"We know he has a cabin around here somewhere," Jeep said, and Bill nodded behind her. "Can you take us there?"

"I can," said Snooger, "but I won't."

"Please?" she asked with her best you'd-be-doing-us-a-favor tone of voice.

"Let's see," the snoggle said. "Three strangers show up in the dead of night, one of them carrying a bongrik, say they're looking for Prince Viktar but they don't really know him, and ask for directions to his place in the swamp even though they don't think he wants company. On top of that, they wake me out of a sound sleep by stepping on my foot. So yes, no, I'm not going to do that."

"The Castle Guard is looking for him," Bill started to say.

"Yes, I know," Snooger said. "And I know you're not helping the Castle Guard because —?"

"They're after us, too," said Jeep.

"Huh." The snoggle looked interested. "Why is that?"

"We're not exactly from around here," Blaine said. "They don't seem to like strangers."

"And I am from around here, but I helped these two, so they're after me now, too," Bill said.

"Why did you help them?" Snooger asked.

Bill looked seriously baffled by the question.

"I don't really know," he conceded. "They're obviously not from around here, and they looked a little lost. I don't turn my back on strangers unless they give me a reason."

"Where are you two from? Argossie?"

"Everybody thinks we're from Argossie," Jeep said.

"It's the accent," Snooger said. "You sound Argossan."

"We're from Earth, actually," she acknowledged. What the heck, being honest worked with Bill Gentle.

"Right. Come on, everyone knows that Earthens are little green people," the snoggle said sarcastically. "Whatever. Let's say you're from Argossie. Why do you care about Prince Viktar anyway?"

It suddenly occurred to Jeep that Snooger was not acting as if he thought the prince was kidnapped, which was the story the Castle Guard was sticking to.

"You do know where he is," she said suddenly. "Otherwise you'd want to help us find him."

"Un-less," the snoggle snorted, "I know he's staying at his secret cabin because it's the safest place to be to get away from it all, and the last thing he wants is strangers who may or may not be allied with the Castle Guard coming to visit in the middle of the night."

"So he is there?" Jeep said, and Snooger jumped back.

"How did you —? That is — No," he insisted. "I'm just telling you a hypothetical situation under which I wouldn't want to help you find the prince."

"Oh, Snooger, will you just shut up and tell me what all the commotion is about?"

This last interruption was spoken by a sudden newcomer to the conversation, a young man in a big floppy robe with some sort of crest sewn into the breast pocket. Jeep, who as you may recall is a young woman, could not help but notice that the disheveled young man was a quite adequate specimen of manhood, with his dark albeit disheveled black hair, his piercing if bleary-eyed brown eyes, his chiseled jaw and high cheekbones.

She had to admit that, at first blush, he was the kind of young man who might serve in a story about a handsome prince.

And by the way Snooger broke into some sort of ritualized motion that might pass for genuflection on Venus, she decided her second blush may be the same as her first.

"Prince Viktar!" she exclaimed softly.

"The same," the handsome prince admitted.

TO BE CONTINUED

KEEPING UP WITH THE THOMPSONS

Thank you for reading *Jeep Thompson & the Lost Prince of Venus: Episode 1: Journey to the Second Planet*! If you enjoyed the ride, I'd appreciate it if you left a review in the appropriate place at your favorite ebook retailer. (You can leave a 1-star review, too, if you hated it, but my appreciation would be a tad muted.) Reviews are important in getting the word out to our fellow readers.

And welcome to my world! You can catch my daily musings at www.warrenbluhm.com — but my semi-monthly newsletter will have regular updates on book projects. You'll be the first to find out when Episode 2 is ready to roll and, once all three episodes are completed, how and when to get the ebook and print editions of the finished novel. Since this story is too big to be contained in a single book, you'll also be the first to know as future installments roll out.

You are getting in on the ground floor of an epic adventure. I'll do my best to keep you entertained and having fun!

Warren Bluhm

www.ingramcontent.com/pod-product-compliance
Lightning Source LLC
LaVergne TN
LVHW061622070526
838199LV00078B/7381